and the
TV CREW

Reading Consultant: Prue Goodwin, Lecturer in literacy and children's books

ORCHARD BOOKS
338 Euston Road, London NW1 3BH
Orchard Books Australia
Level 17/207 Kent Street, Sydney, NSW 2000

First published in 2012
First paperback publication in 2013

ISBN 978 1 40831 335 0 (hardback)
ISBN 978 1 40831 343 5 (paperback)

Text © Justine Smith 2012
Illustrations © Clare Elsom 2012

1 3 5 7 9 10 8 6 4 2 (hardback)
1 3 5 7 9 10 8 6 4 2 (paperback)

Printed in China

Orchard Books is a division of Hachette Children's Books,
an Hachette UK company.
www.hachette.co.uk

and the
TV CREW

Justine Smith • Clare Elsom

ORCHARD

Zak Zoo lives at Number One, Africa Avenue.
His mum and dad are away on
safari, so his animal family is looking
after him. Sometimes things get a little . . .

. . . WILD!

Pam

Dad

Mum

Emily

Zak

Nanny
Hilda

Bob

Charlie

Tom

Bill

Every time Zak Zoo went to the shops, crowds followed him. Zak was getting famous for having an animal family.

At first Zak didn't mind being a celebrity. He liked it and so did his animal family.

Zak was often in the newspaper.
He liked to cut out the articles
about him and send them to
his parents.

Dear Mum and Dad,
Look! I am in the
paper again.
Love, Zak

P.S. Good news! I
remembered to brush
my teeth last week.

Mr and Mrs Zoo were very impressed. They hung up all Zak's newspaper cuttings in their jungle camp.

The whole world had started to talk about Zak Zoo. Very soon, a TV crew arrived!

They set up their cameras and
lights, and started to film Zak.
"Tell us about you," they said.
"Tell us about Zak Zoo."

At first, Zak liked being filmed,

and so did his animal family.

Nanny Hilda especially enjoyed being in front of the cameras.

But Zak and his animal family began to get tired of celebrity life, because the TV crew never left them alone. They filmed day and night.

The TV crew wanted to film everything, and they didn't care whether Zak was happy about it, or not.

Zak was not the only one who was unhappy. The animals were giving the TV crew problems.

After Bill the buffalo ate the microphone, the TV crew packed up and left. Everyone was very glad to see them go.

"That's that!" said Zak. "Back to
normal life!"

Now that the TV crew was gone, life was quiet. Zak Zoo was happy to be normal again and most of his animal family was happy too.

Only Nanny Hilda missed being famous. She started writing a blog called "My Life with Zak Zoo".

Now that the TV crew had finished, "The Zak Zoo Show" was shown on TV! Every Friday night the Zoo family watched it.

The show was very popular.

Far away in the jungle, even Zak's mum and dad watched the show.

But there was a problem – now
that Zak was on TV, he was even
more famous. His fans started
camping in the garden.

Then the TV crew called and
asked Zak if they could come and
film "Zak Zoo, Series Two".

Zak did not want to be a celebrity any more.

"I know what to do!" he said. He wrote a note to his mum and dad, and gave it to Tom the post-bird.

Mr and Mrs Zoo came right away.

When the TV crew arrived to film "Zak Zoo, Series Two", Bill the Buffalo was waiting.

There was a letter pinned to the front door.

Dear TV Crew,

Sorry, we are not in. We are

on holiday.

Love, Zak Zoo

P.S. Bill is guarding the house.

P.P.S. We have thrown

 ← Bill   away the TV.

Written by Justine Smith • Illustrated by Clare Elsom

All priced at £4.99

Orchard Books are available from all good bookshops,
or can be ordered from our website: www.orchardbooks.co.uk,
or telephone 01235 827702, or fax 01235 827703.

Prices and availability are subject to change.